LAURENCE YEP

The Butterfly Boy

Pictures by
JEANNE M. LEE

FARRAR STRAUS GIROUX   New York

*T*here once was a boy who dreamed he was a butterfly,
and, as a butterfly, he always dreamed he was a boy.
And this would sometimes get him into trouble.
Because sometimes he would forget he was a boy
and think he was a butterfly.

Once a buffalo blocked the road,
    so the boy tried to fly over him
and wound up on the buffalo's back instead.
And the buffalo carried him for three miles
    while the boy lay on his stomach, flapping his arms.
And, laughing and joking, everyone fell in step behind him
    and called it the butterfly's parade.
    And the buffalo carried him right into the city.

There he saw the butterflies
    embroidered on a lady's robe
    and they looked so real
    that he jumped off the buffalo
    and tried to dance with them,
        and got hit on the nose with her fan.

And as he stood in the market
he heard people shouting about their fresh fish,
        shouting about their vegetables,
        shouting about their flowers,
and he became hungry,
        but like a butterfly rather than a boy,
and he put his face to the flowers
        and tried to suck the nectar.

But whenever he made a fool of himself,
the laughter of the others only sounded like
the roaring of a wind,
carrying him higher and higher toward the sun,
the sun,
the sun,
the warmth of the sun,
hugging the warmth with rainbow wings,

and then dancing,
     dancing in a ragged, coarse robe,
     dancing and drumming on his thighs
     to the clicking of the cicadas.
And the more they laughed,
     the higher he flew
        and the faster he danced
     right out of the city and back to his tiny house
        with boards held together by vines
        and a door made of brambles.
The world was like a book to him,
     and the fields and hills,
     the rivers and lakes,
        were like pages full of words
        —words that he understood as a butterfly
        but not as a boy.

As a butterfly, he would sit upon a flower
        watching the morning mists drifting along the river
        and remembering people's shadows
        slipping along city streets,
                so lonely,
                so tired,
        melting into the cold shadows of banks and palaces,
                of forts and prisons.
And he would feel sorry for the others
        who could not see with butterfly eyes.

As a boy, he could stand for hours staring into a puddle
because he saw the rainbow shining on the surface
like a skin shed by a snake,
like the ghost of a seashell.

When someone asked why he was staring at scum,
he tried and tried to explain,
    but he could only talk of snakes and seashells.
So everyone thought he was stupid
    because he couldn't see how ugly things were.
And he was sorry for the others
    who did not understand.

And yet, either as a boy or as a butterfly,
    he did not understand many things that people did.
Once a great lord invaded their land.
And before him marched his mighty army
    with spear points gleaming like a river of stars.
Frightened, the other people knelt
    and bowed their heads against the dirt,
    for the lord's army made the ground tremble
    like an earthquake.
But the Butterfly Boy only stood and laughed,
for all the marching legs reminded him of a centipede
    hurrying along through the grass,
    thinking it was so important because it had so many legs.
And the lord became angry when he heard the Butterfly Boy
    and ordered his soldiers to seize the insolent child.

And when the soldiers led the boy before their lord,
    the boy began to weep.
Instantly, the lord felt better.
    "Are you afraid of me now?"
But the boy had seen the lord with his butterfly eyes:
    and the lord in his armor reminded him
    of a beetle on its back, wriggling its legs.
"I'm only sad for you," the boy said, "and all your other little bugs."
    And the lord ordered his men to let the boy go.
"He is either a madman or a prophet," the lord said. "And I have no
    quarrel with either."

Winter came early and the lord and his army perished in the snow.
So there was a great celebration with feasting and fireworks.
And everyone remembered the Butterfly Boy,
so they made him guest of honor
and called him brave and wise.
But praise meant no more to him than insults
and the fireworks reminded him of the lovely flowers
that had vanished.
And the sound of footsteps in the snow,
so crisp,
so cold,
reminded him of the end of flying
and the end of life.

So he ran back to his house
and shuffled inside, feeling very, very sad,
and thinking,
    "Maybe the others are right.
    Maybe I am a fool."
But at New Year's,
    in the midst of the cold and the dark and the snow,
    the wild plum tree flowered outside his house.
And the scent of its pink blossoms,
    so sharp,
    so sweet,
        slipped through his flimsy walls
and reminded him that all things return
and that the snow was a giant cocoon
    for the rebirth of the world.

And, as a boy,
he ran out into the winter snow
and flitted about through a rain of pink petals
like a butterfly floating through the flowers.

And, as a butterfly,
he flew into a summer meadow
and hopped and skipped among the flowers
like a boy dancing in the snow.

There once was a boy who dreamed he was a butterfly, and, as a butterfly, he always dreamed he was a boy, and he was never sure which he liked better.

AFTERWORD

The story and images are drawn from the writings of Chuang Tzu, sometimes called the Butterfly Philosopher, who lived in China during the troubled times at the end of the fourth century B.C.

To Bill Broder, who balances many lives
LY

In memory of Sibyl Belmont
JML

Text copyright © 1993 by Laurence Yep
Pictures copyright © 1993 by Jeanne M. Lee
All rights reserved
Library of Congress catalog card number: 92-54644
Published simultaneously in Canada by HarperCollinsCanadaLtd
Color separations by Imago Publishing Ltd.
Printed and bound in the United States of America
by Berryville Graphics
Designed by Martha Rago
First edition, 1993